☐ **W9-BBW-515**

SMYTHE GAMBRELL LIBRARY
WESTMINSTER ELEMENTARY SCHOOLS
1424 WEST PACES FERRY RD., N. W.
ATLANTA, GA. 30327

RUMPELSTILTSKIN

A Tale Told Long Ago by the Brothers Grimm

Retold by Edith Tarcov
Pictures by Edward Gorey

Four Winds Press   New York

SMYTHE GAMBRELL LIBRARY
WESTMINSTER ELEMENTARY SCHOOLS
1424 WEST PACES FERRY RD., N. W.
ATLANTA, GA. 30327 .

J
398
Grimm

LIBRARY OF CONGRESS CATALOGING IN PUBLICATION DATA
TARCOV, EDITH.
RUMPELSTILTSKIN.
SUMMARY: A STRANGE LITTLE MAN HELPS THE MILLER'S
DAUGHTER SPIN STRAW INTO GOLD FOR THE KING ON THE CON-
DITION THAT SHE WILL GIVE HIM HER FIRST-BORN CHILD.
[1. FAIRY TALES. 2. FOLKLORE—GERMANY] 1. GOREY, EDWARD
ST. JOHN, ILLUS. II. GRIMM, JACOB LUDWIG, 1785-1863. RUM-
PELSTILZSCHEN. III. TITLE.
PZ8.T175RU   398.21'0943   74-2139
            ISBN 0-590-07393-1

PUBLISHED BY FOUR WINDS PRESS
A DIVISION OF SCHOLASTIC MAGAZINES, INC., NEW YORK, N.Y.
TEXT COPYRIGHT © 1973 BY EDITH TARCOV
ILLUSTRATIONS COPYRIGHT © 1973 BY EDWARD GOREY
ALL RIGHTS RESERVED
PRINTED IN THE UNITED STATES OF AMERICA
LIBRARY OF CONGRESS CATALOG CARD NUMBER: 74-2139
1 2 3 4 5 78 77 76 75 74

To Joshua

16229

Once upon a time there was a poor miller
who had a beautiful daughter.

One morning, the king came riding by.

He stopped to talk to the miller.

The miller wanted to say something interesting.

So he said: "King, I have a daughter — "

"I suppose she is beautiful," said the king.

"Oh yes. She is beautiful," the miller said.
"But she is more than that. My daughter . . .
MY daughter . . . can spin straw into gold!"

"Spin straw into gold?" said the king.
"Hm. Well! Tell your daughter to come to me
this evening."

That evening the miller's daughter
came to the king.

The king took her into a little room.

There was nothing in the room but

    a heap of straw,

    a chair,

    and a spinning wheel.

"Now spin," said the king.
"If you do not spin all this straw into gold
by morning, you must die."

The king locked the door and went away.

Now the poor miller's daughter was all alone.
She really did not know how
to spin straw into gold.
She did not know what to do.
So she began to cry.

Suddenly the door opened,
and a tiny little man came in.
"Good evening, miller's daughter,"
he said. "Why are you crying?"

"Oh!" she said. "Oh! The king told me
to spin all this straw into gold.
If it's not done by morning,
I must die!"

"What will you give me
if I do it for you?" the little man asked.

"I will give you my necklace," said the
miller's daughter.

The little man took the necklace.
Then he sat down at the spinning wheel.

Whirl! Whirl! Whirl!
Three times he whirled the wheel
and the work was done.

Now that heap of straw
was a heap of gold.
And the little man went away.

As soon as the sun was up,
the king came in.
He looked at the heap of gold.
The king was pleased.

"You have done well,"
he said to the miller's daughter.
"But I need more gold than that."

That evening the king took the miller's daughter
into a bigger room.
There was nothing in that room but

    a chair,

    a spinning wheel,

    and a great big heap of straw.

"Now spin," said the king.
"If you do not spin all this straw into gold
by morning, you must die."

The king locked the door and went away.

Again the poor miller's daughter was all alone.
She looked at all that straw.
She did not know what to do.
So she began to cry.

Again the door opened
and the little man came in.

"Good evening, miller's daughter,"
he said. "What will you give me
if I spin all this straw into gold?"

"I will give you my ring," said the miller's daughter.

The little man took the ring.
Then he sat down at the spinning wheel.

Whirl! Whirl! Whirl!
Three times he whirled the wheel
and the work was done.

Now that great big heap of straw
was a great big heap of gold.
And the little man went away.

As soon as the sun was up,

the king came in.

He looked at that great big heap of gold.

The king was pleased.

"You have done well,"

he said to the miller's daughter.

"But I need more gold than that."

That evening the king took the miller's daughter
into a very big room.
There was nothing in that room but
    a chair,
    a spinning wheel,
    and heaps and heaps of straw!

"Now spin," said the king. "If you spin
all this straw into gold by morning,
you will be my wife."

The king locked the door and went away.

When the miller's daughter was all alone,
the little man came again.
Again he said, "Good evening, miller's daughter.
What will you give me
if I spin this straw into gold?"

"I gave you my necklace," she said.
"And I gave you my ring.
I have nothing left to give you."

"Nothing?" the little man asked.

"Nothing," said the miller's daughter.
And she began to cry.

"Don't cry, miller's daughter,"
the little man said. "I will help you.
But
you must promise to give me something. . . ."

"Anything! Anything you ask!" she cried.

"Then promise me," the little man said.
"Promise me that when you are queen
you will give me your first baby."

"Yes! Yes! I promise!"
said the miller's daughter. And she thought,
"Who knows if I really shall be queen?
And if I am queen, who knows
if I shall have a baby?"

"Yes! Yes!" she said again. "I promise!"

The little man sat down at the spinning wheel.

Whirl! Whirl! Whirl!
Three times he whirled the wheel
and the work was done.

Now those heaps and heaps of straw
were heaps and heaps of gold.
And the little man went away.

As soon as the sun was up

the king came in.

He looked at the heaps and heaps of gold.

The king was very pleased.

He looked at the miller's beautiful daughter.

"My dear," said the king.

"We will be married this very day!"

And so the miller's daughter became queen.

A year later, the king and the queen
had a beautiful baby.

One evening the queen was in her room,
playing with her baby.
Suddenly,
the little man came into her room.

"Good evening, queen," he said. "Now give me
what you promised."

The queen had forgotten the little man.
She had forgotten her promise, too.

"What promise?" she asked.

"You promised to give me
your first baby," said the little man.

"I cannot give you my baby," said the queen.
"I will give you my golden necklace."
But the little man shook his head.

"I will give you my golden necklace
and my beautiful golden ring," said the queen.
But the little man shook his head.

"You may have all the riches of the kingdom,"
she said. "But let me keep my baby."

"No, queen," said the little man.
"A baby is dearer to me
than all the riches of the world."

The queen began to cry.

The little man looked at the queen.
"I will give you three days," he said.
"If in three days you know my name,
you may keep your baby.
I will come every evening, for three evenings.
Each time I will ask if you know my name."

And the little man went away.

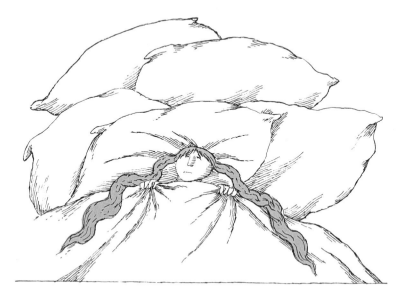

That night the poor queen could not sleep.

As soon as the sun was up, the queen
called for her messenger. "Messenger,"
she said. "Go through the town.
Find out all the names people have.
Come back before evening
and tell them all to me."

That evening, the little man came
into the queen's room.
"Good evening, queen," he said.
"Do you know my name?"

The queen tried all the many names
her messenger had found.

"Is it Al?" she asked.

        "No," said the little man.

        "That's not my name."

"Is it Bill?"

        "No."

"Is it Charlie?"

           "No."

"Is it Dan?"

        "No."

"Is it Ed?"

      "No."

"Is it Fred?"

      "No."

"Is it George?"

      "No."

"Is it Henry?"

      "No. No, no. That's not my name."

So they went, on and on and on.

But all the little man said was:

"No. No, no. That's not my name."

That very evening,

as soon as the little man had gone away,

the queen called for her messenger.

"Messenger," she said. "Go through the kingdom.

Find out all the strange names people have.

Come back tomorrow, before evening,

and tell them all to me. Hurry."

On the second evening the little man
came into the queen's room.
"Good evening, queen," he said.
"Do you know my name?"

The queen asked him all the strange names
her messenger had found.

"Is it Angel Face?" she asked.

"No," said the little man.
"That's not my name."

"Is it Bump-on-a-Lump?"

"No."

"Is it Diddle Dump?"

"No."

"Is it Bottom?"

"No."

"Is it Top?"

"No."

"Is it Skip?"

"No."

"Is it Hop?"

"No."

"Is it Goldie Locks?"

"No."

"Is it Lucky Fox?"

"No."

"Is it Bluster Beast?"

"No. No, no. That's not my name."

So they went, on and on and on.

But all the little man said was:
"No. No, no. That's not my name."

That evening,
as soon as the little man had gone away,
the queen called for her messenger.
"Messenger," she said. "Go once more
through the kingdom.
You must find more names for me!
Come back tomorrow, before evening,
and tell them all to me. Hurry!"

On the third day, it was almost evening
when the messenger came back.

"I could not find any new names for you,"
he said.

"Not any new names?" asked the queen.
"Not any new names at all?"

"Well," said the messenger. "I did find
something. Something very strange. . ."

"Tell me," said the queen. "And hurry!"

So the messenger told the queen what he had found.

"Last night," he said, "I went up high,
high into the mountains.
I went deep into the woods
where the fox and the hare say good night
to each other. There I saw a little house.
In front of that little house there was a fire.
And around that little fire
a tiny little man was dancing.
While he was dancing, he was singing:

Tonight my cakes I bake.

Tonight my beer I make.

Tomorrow, tomorrow, tomorrow

The queen's little baby I take!

Lucky I'll go as lucky I came

for R U M P E L S T I L T S K I N is my name!

How happy the queen was to hear that name!

Now it was the third evening,
and the little man came again.

"Good evening, queen," he said.
"Do you know my name?"

"Tell me, is it Tom?" the queen asked.

"No."

"Hm . . . let me see. Is it Dick?"

"No."

"Well, let me think. . . . Is it Harry?"

"No." The little man laughed and he shook his head.
"No, no. That's not my name."

"Then . . . tell me . . ." asked the queen.

"Could it be . . . ?

Is it . . .

perhaps . . .

R U M P E L S T I L T S K I N ?"

How angry the little man was!
"The devil must have told you!" he cried.
"The devil himself!"

And he stamped so hard
with his right foot
that he made a deep hole in the floor.

Oh, he was angry!
He stamped hard with his left foot, too.
And he fell deep into the earth.

No one has seen him since.

SMYTHE GAMBRELL LIBRARY
WESTMINSTER ELEMENTARY SCHOOLS
1424 WEST PACES FERRY RD., N. W.
ATLANTA, GA. 30327